Milly and Molly

For my grandchildren
Thomas, Harry, Ella and Madeleine

Milly, Molly and Different Dads

Copyright © Milly Molly Books, 2002

Gill Pittar and Cris Morrell assert the moral right to
be recognized as the author and illustrator of this
work.

Published by
Milly Molly Books
P O Box 539
Gisborne, New Zealand
email: books@millymolly.com

Printed by Rhythm Consolidated Berhad, Malaysia

ISBN: 1-86972-019-9

10   9   8   7   6   5   4   3   2   1

Milly, Molly
and
Different Dads

"We may look different
but we feel the same."

It was a cold, wet, winter morning.
Miss Blythe asked everyone to take off
their wet shoes and put them by the heater.

"Come on, let's get warm," she said,
rubbing her hands firmly together.

No one had missed Sophie until, slowly,
the door opened.

Sophie stood dripping. It was hard to
tell whether her face was wet with tears
or raindrops.

"Come here, Sophie," Miss Blythe said gently.
"Let's take off your wet coat and shoes."

"Can you tell us what's happened?"

"Dad packed his suitcase and left home," sobbed Sophie.

Miss Blythe held Sophie against her
warm cardigan and said softly,
"Let's talk about our dads."

"My dad's in the hospital," started Jack.

"I've got two dads," said Elizabeth.

"I've only got one dad," said Milly.

"My dad's away with the Army and I
only see him sometimes," Harry added.

"My dad's at home every day," slipped in Tom.

"I go and stay with dad for holidays because
he has another family now," said Poppy.

"My dad's in a wheelchair," stated Humphrey.

"Dad adopted me when I was one," said Molly.

"Uncle Stan looks after me like a dad,"
added George thoughtfully.

"My dad is blind," said Meg.

"Dad died last year," Alf said quietly.

"And my dad died when I was six,"
confided Miss Blythe.

Sophie squeezed in between Milly and Molly.

"My dad is deaf," she said softly.

"So there we are," Miss Blythe said.
"All dads and families are different.
That's just the way it is."

Milly, Molly and Different Dads

The value implicitly expressed in this story is 'acceptance of family diversity' - to understand and accept that all families are different.

Miss Blythe encourages the class to share their dads differences to help Sophie accept that all families are different.

"We *may* look different but we feel the same."

B O O K S

Other picture books in the Milly, Molly series include: